BIG HEROES!

By Billy Wrecks
Illustrated by Dan Schoening

 A GOLDEN BOOK • NEW YORK

DC SUPER FRIENDS and all related titles, characters, and elements are trademarks of DC Comics. Copyright © 2011 DC Comics.
All rights reserved. Published in the United States by Golden Books, an imprint of Random House Children's Books, a division of Random House, Inc., 1745 Broadway, New York, NY 10019, and in Canada by Random House of Canada Limited, Toronto. Golden Books, A Golden Book, A Little Golden Book, the G colophon, and the distinctive gold spine are registered trademarks of Random House, Inc.

www.randomhouse.com/kids

Educators and librarians, for a variety of teaching tools, visit us at www.randomhouse.com/teachers

Library of Congress Control Number: 2010927312

ISBN: 978-0-375-87237-2

Printed in the United States of America

Random House Children's Books supports the First Amendment and celebrates the right to read.

10 9 8 7

Trouble comes in many shapes and sizes, but no trouble is too big for the world's mightiest heroes. When the Flash, Aquaman, Green Lantern, Superman, and Batman unite to save the day, they are known as the **Super Friends**!

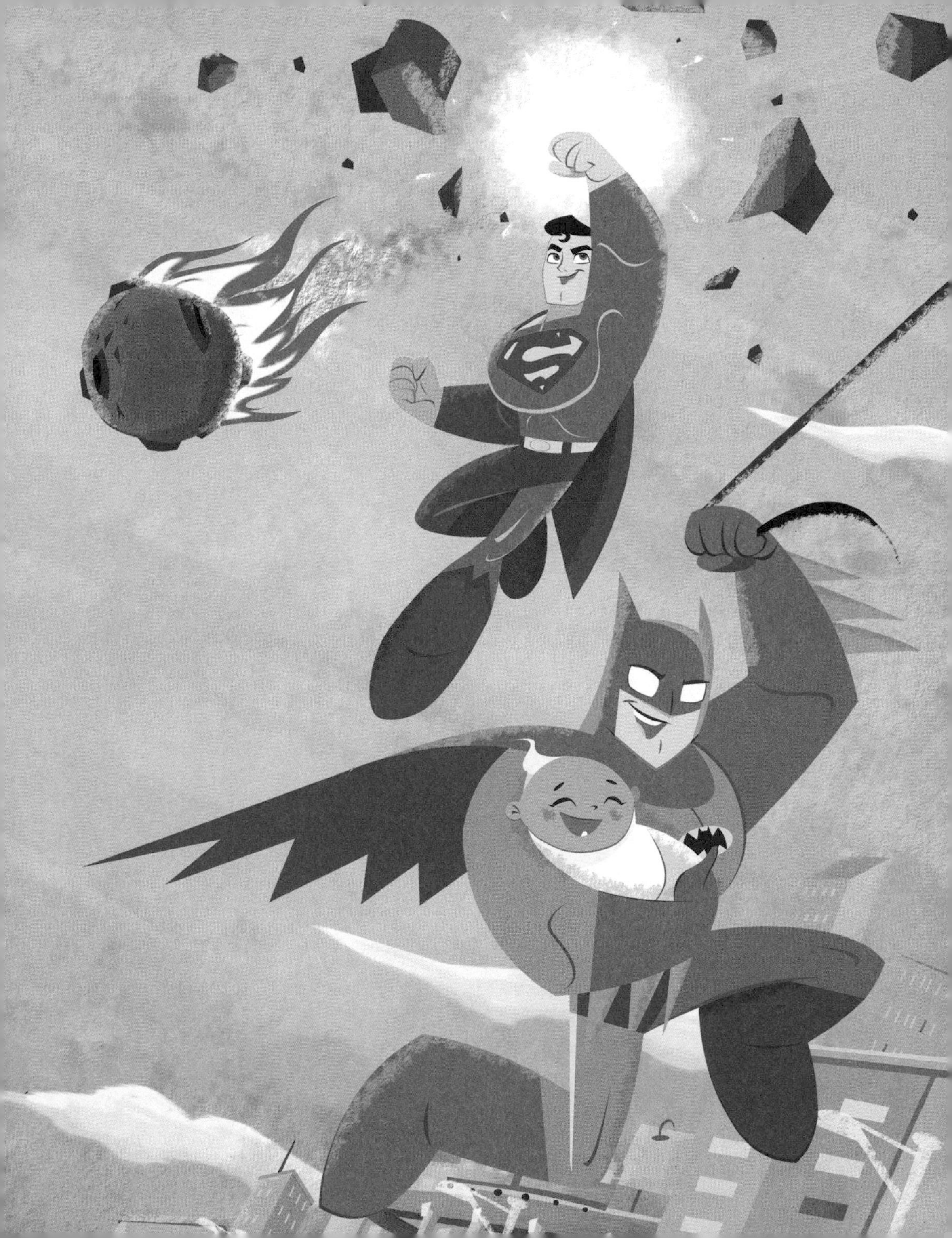

After the Super Friends saved Metropolis once again, the city thanked them with a loud cheer. But one person was not cheering—

Lex Luthor!

"My latest invention will bring those Super Friends down to size," the villain grumbled in his secret laboratory. "I am going to zap them with my . . .

. . . **SHRINK** RAY!"

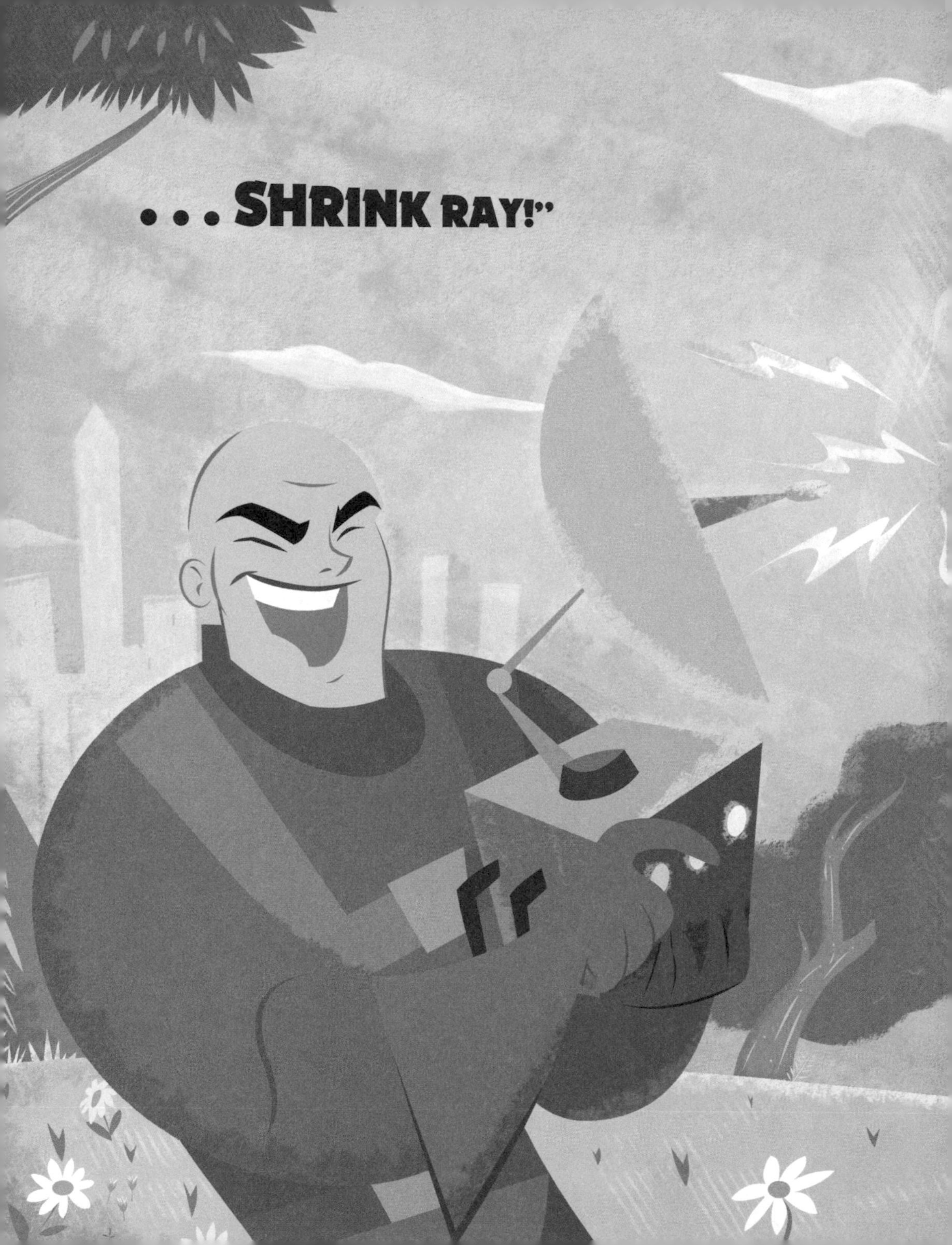

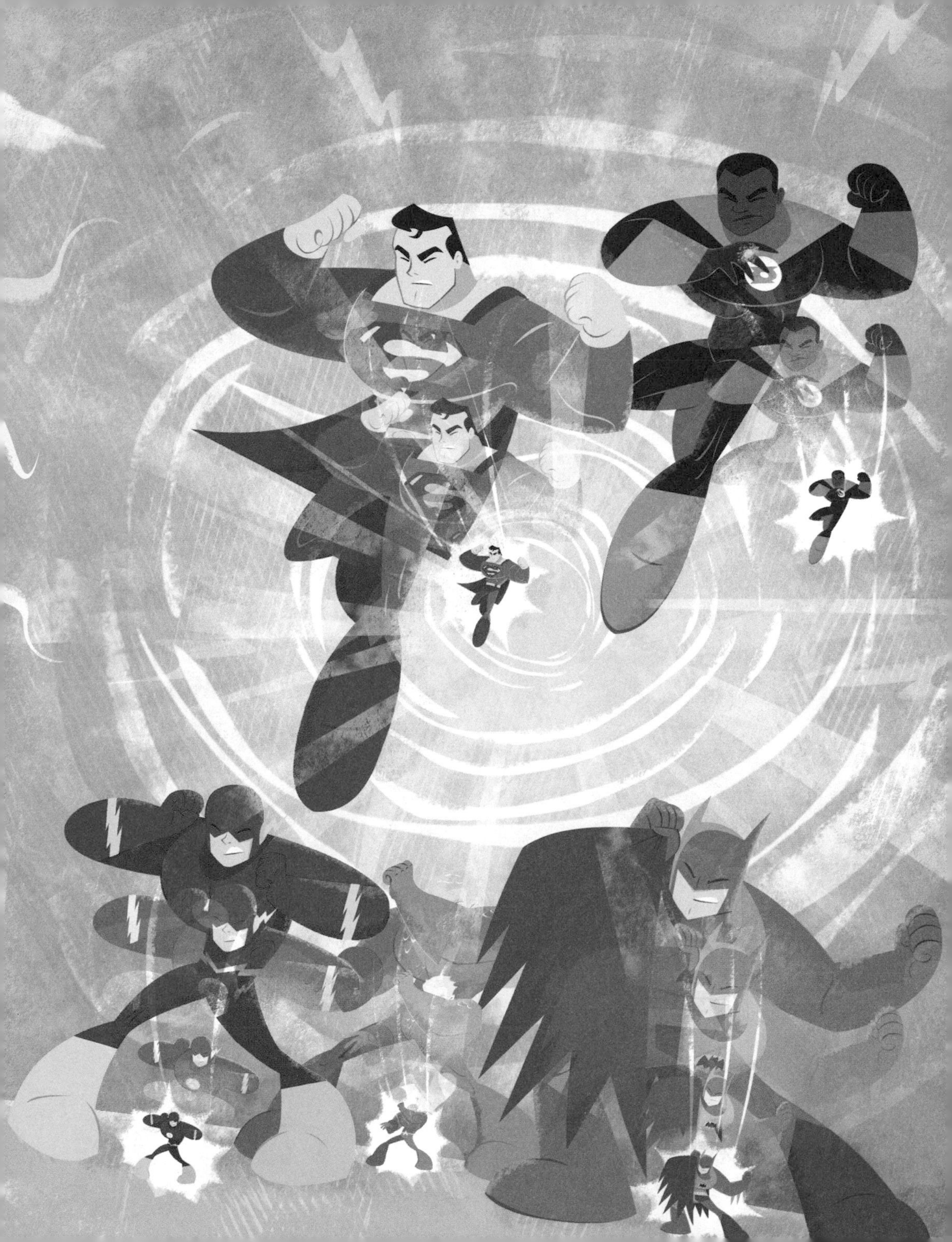

"Now nothing will stop me from taking over Metropolis!" Lex shouted.

The colossal criminal took a deep breath—and blew the shrunken Super Friends away!

"We're the size of ants!" Batman said.
"But we can still stop Lex!" Superman declared.
Only the Flash noticed the dark shadow looming
over their heads!

Suddenly, an enormous praying mantis grabbed Superman in its spiky claws. The Super Friends began to battle the insect!

"We need a little help from one of Mother Nature's other creatures," Batman said. He threw himself against a spider's web, causing the silky strands to vibrate.

A hairy spider scurried down the web and attacked the praying mantis! As the two creepy-crawlies clashed, the Super Friends dashed away.

Unfortunately, the Flash ran right into
a hungry Venus flytrap. The plant's prickly
jaws **SNAPPED** shut, trapping the Flash!

Superman used his incredible strength
to open the plant's thorny mouth. Batman
swung in on his Batrope to free the Flash.
"Thanks," the Flash said. "For a second,
I thought I was going to be fast food!"

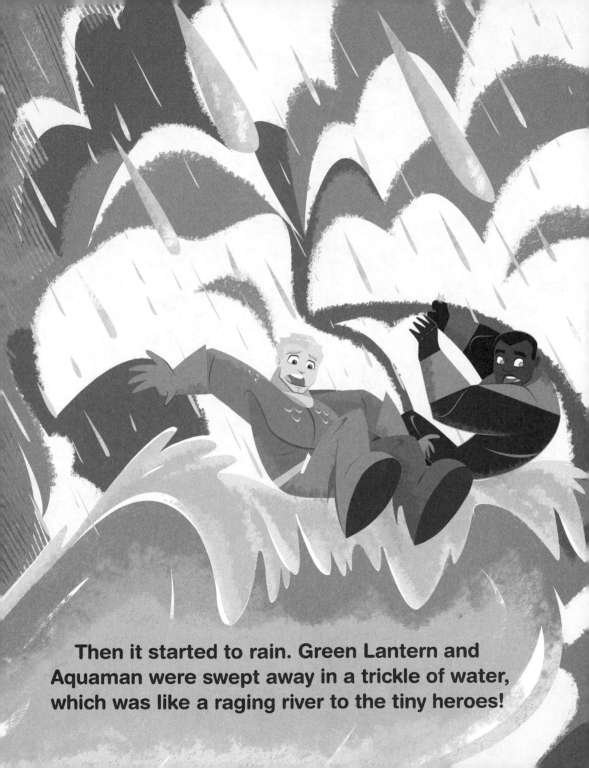

Then it started to rain. Green Lantern and Aquaman were swept away in a trickle of water, which was like a raging river to the tiny heroes!

As Aquaman tumbled under the water, he called out to a nearby turtle. It gave him a ride to solid ground.

The other Super Friends dodged raindrops as they raced to catch up with Aquaman.

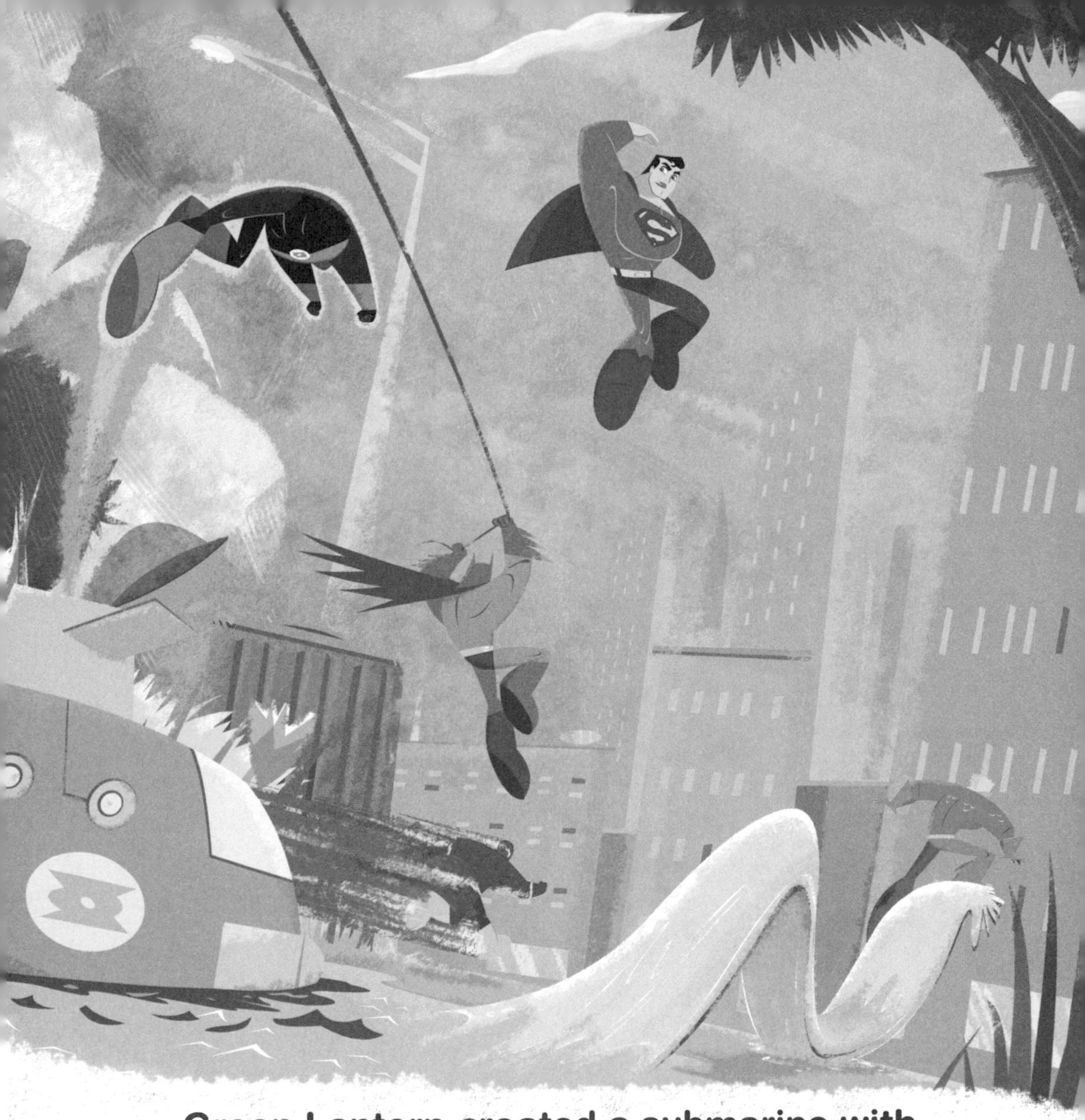

Green Lantern created a submarine with his power ring to escape the rough water.

"Let's go get Lex Luthor," Superman said as all the Super Friends arrived safely on the scene.

The shrunken heroes dodged speeding cars . . .

barking dogs . . .

sticky fingers . . .

and big boots . . .

until they found Lex.

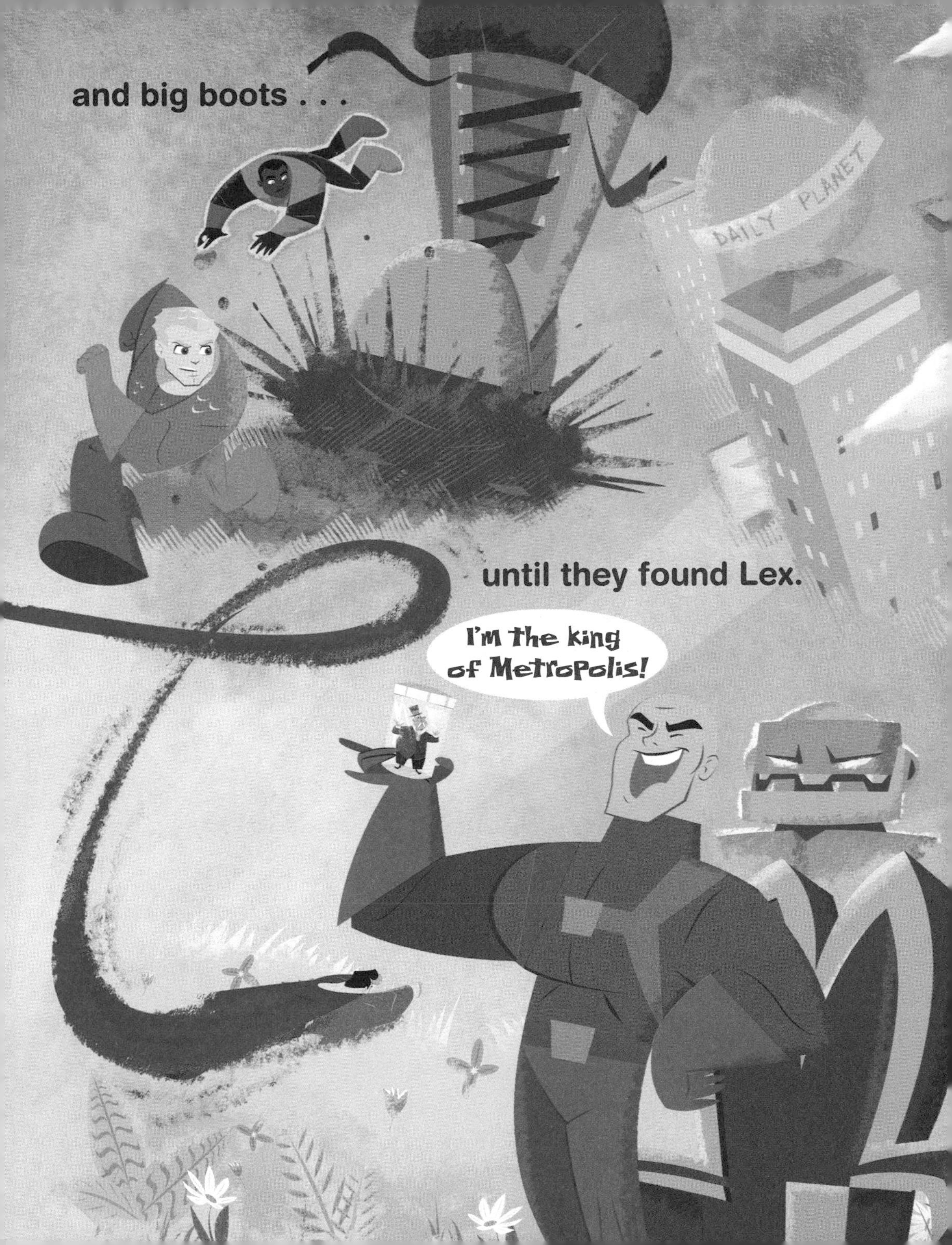
DAILY PLANET
I'm the king of Metropolis!

Lex didn't notice a hornets' nest hanging over his head. But the Super Friends did!

Superman used his heat vision to cut the nest loose.

It fell right into Lex's lap! Hundreds of angry hornets started to sting him.

At super-speed, the Flash ran to the shrink ray and switched the controls to reverse.

Green Lantern used his power ring to activate the shrink ray. The Super Friends began to grow bigger and bigger and . . .

BIGGER!

Superman grabbed Lex. The people of
Metropolis were saved. Everyone cheered!

"Foiled again, Lex," Batman said. "And this time by a bunch of tiny hornets."

"It just goes to show you," Superman said, "that heroes will always save the day—no matter what size they are!"